For Wren, our little outside heart on a string. – C.A.

For Ryan. Our love will always stretch to reach. – K.B.

Quarto is the authority on a wide range of topics.

Quarto educates, entertains and enriches the lives of our readers—enthusiasts and lovers of hands-on living.

www.quartoknows.com

First published in 2020 by words & pictures,
an imprint of The Quarto Group.
26391 Crown Valley Parkway, Suite 220
Mission Viejo, CA 92691, USA
T: +1 949 380 7510
F: +1 949 380 7575
www.QuartoKnows.com

A CIP record for this book is available from the Library of Congress.

ISBN: 978 0 7112 5547 0

Manufactured in Guangzhou, China EB032021

9 8 7 6 5 4 3 2

CORRINNE
AVERISS

KIRSTI
BEAUTYMAN

love

words & pictures

Everyone loved everyone in Tess's house.

Daddy loved Mommy, Mommy loved Daddy.
Tess loved Mommy and Daddy and Tom.
Everyone loved Tom, and Tom loved everyone else...

...apart from Diggle,
who barked loudly and
scared him sometimes.

But Diggle loved everyone too.

Mom said, "Loving someone means
you like being near them.
As near as you can possibly get!"

Tess thought about all the love that filled their home, like the light inside one of Daddy's little houses.

If Tess had to leave home, then
Mommy or Daddy went with her.

And so the love came too
—wherever she went—and
kept her warm, like a scarf.

When Tess visited Granny and Gramps's house, the love she had left there last time was still safe inside.

Tess always had love nearby.

But one sunny September day,
it was time for Tess to start school.

Mommy and Daddy couldn't come to school.
Tom was too little, Granny and Gramps were too big...

...and dogs can't use crayons.

So Tess would have to be brave all by herself.

School was large, with lots of doors and windows.
It wasn't like a candle house or a warm scarf.

"If we're not together, will the love still find me?" asked Tess.

"Don't worry," said Mom. "Love is like a string between us—it can stretch as far as it needs to."

They said goodbye at the gate.

It felt strange to Tess,
not having love near.

How could she
know that
Mommy was
on the end of
her string?

She tugged, but perhaps
Mommy was already too
far away to feel it.

Tess ran right up to the school gate.
She might be closer that way.

She tugged again.

"Are you okay, Tess?" A teacher had joined her.

"I don't know if Mommy is on the end of my string," Tess explained.
The teacher gave Tess a hug. She was named Mrs. Turley, and
she understood.

"I promise, your Mommy is
always on the end!" she said.

As they walked back to the classroom,
Tess noticed a little thread between them.

That felt nice.

Mrs. Turley guided Tess to a table, where
a boy was making a paper dragon.
"Do you want to help?" he asked,
and offered her the glue.

As they played, Tess told the boy all about her strings.
"I have strings too!" said the boy, excitedly.

He was named Harry and one of his strings
was very special. It stretched far away because
his daddy had died when he was small.
"It goes up, up high," Harry explained.

Now Tess had a string with her new friend, too.

The more she looked, the more
Tess saw that everyone had strings.

Love that went
sideways, backward,
forward, and upward.

When school ended, she felt a little tug
on her string as she thought about
Mommy waiting for her at the gate.

Tess stood with Mrs. Turley and
watched, as one by one, all the
children were met with a hug
and left for home.

Where was her Mommy?
Tess's tummy fluttered
and her heart beat fast.
Her sadness turned to worry.
And she tugged the string again
and again to see if anyone was there.

Mrs. Turley took her back into the classroom to wait. It seemed to Tess that her string was useless.

IT WASN'T CONNECTING HER TO ANYTHING!

With trembling hands, she untied
the knot and let it fall to the floor.

Then Tess cried and cried, and
though Mrs. Turley tried to help,
she wanted to be alone.

Suddenly she felt a hand
on her shoulder ... Mommy!

"I'm so sorry Tess. Tom was
crying for his lost teddy.
It took us ages to find it!"
Tess hugged Mommy tightly.

Then she remembered
what she had done.
"I untied our string!"
Tess confessed, sadly.

"Well, let's fix that," said Mommy, smiling. She looped the string, pulled the knot, and reconnected them.

Everything felt right again.
"I promise you Tess, our string may stretch or
tangle, but it will never truly break," said Mommy.

Then Mommy and Tess cried happy tears,
and felt their love wrap them in a big bundle ...

... and roll them all the way home.